JOHN WORSLEY

The illustrations by John Worsley in the *Golden Classics* series, have greatly added to the impact and charm of these dramatic stories. Now well-established as a portrait painter and marine artist, John Worsley was in the Royal Navy during the war. Taken prisoner, he and a fellow officer constructed an astonishingly life-like dummy to help in their escape plan. After the war he was appointed adviser to the makers of the famous war film, *Albert RN*, which tells the true story of this remarkable feat.

Robert Louis Stevenson's
TREASURE ISLAND

Retold by Jane Carruth

GOLDEN PRESS · NEW YORK
Western Publishing Company, Inc.
Racine, Wisconsin

Copyright © 1975 ibp Intercontinental Book Productions
U.S. edition published 1975 by Golden Press, New York. Western Publishing Company, Inc.
All rights reserved. Golden, A Golden Book ® and Golden Press ® are trademarks of Western Publishing Company, Inc.
Library of Congress Catalog Card Number: 74-33820
ISBN 0 307 14750 9
Printed in Italy.

The old sea dog

SQUIRE TRELAWNEY, Doctor Livesey, and the rest of those gentlemen have asked me to write down the whole particulars about Treasure Island, from the beginning to the end. So I take up my pen and go back to the time when my father kept the 'Admiral Benbow' inn, and the days of the brown old seaman with the saber scar, who took up lodgings under our roof.

I remember him as if it were yesterday, as he came plodding to the inn door, pulling his sea chest behind him in a hand barrow. A tall, strong, heavy, nut-brown man; his thick pigtail falling over the shoulders of his soiled blue coat; his hands ragged and calloused, with black, broken nails; and the saber scar across one cheek, a dirty, livid white.

I remember him looking round the cove where our inn stood and whistling to himself as he did so. Then he broke out into that old sea song that he sang so often afterwards:

"Fifteen men on the dead man's chest —
Yo-ho-ho, and a bottle of rum!"

Coming to the inn, he rapped on the door with a bit of stick like a hand-spike that he carried, and when my father appeared, called roughly for a glass of rum.

"This is a handy cove," he said to my father, at last. "Much company, mate?"

My father replied no, there was very little company. More was the pity.

"Then I'll stay here a bit," the seaman continued. "I'm a plain man; rum and bacon and eggs is all I want." And he threw down three or four gold pieces. "You can call me Captain."

The Captain was a very silent man. All day he wandered around the cove, or stood upon the cliffs, with a brass telescope. Each evening, he sat in a corner of the parlor, drinking rum with a little water. Whenever a seaman put up at the 'Admiral Benbow,' as sometimes happened, he would look at him for a long time through the curtained door before he entered the parlor; and he was always sure to be particularly silent, when any stranger was present.

In the first week, he promised me a silver fourpenny on the first of every month if I would only keep my "weather-eye open for a seafaring man with one leg," and let him know the moment he appeared. From his tone, I guessed that he held this man in great fear.

All the time the Captain lived with us he made no change whatever in his dress. I remember so well the appearance of his coat, which he patched himself upstairs in his room, and which, before the end, was in rags. After some months, he stopped paying for his keep and my father dared not ask him for money.

Poor father, he was far from well now and our good friend, Dr. Livesey, came quite often to see him. Afterwards he would talk quietly to my mother in the parlor.

The contrast between the neat, kindly doctor with his white powdered wig and his bright eyes and the filthy, heavy, scarecrow of a seaman was striking. I remember how late one afternoon the doctor came to see my father and then went into the parlor to talk with my mother.

The Captain was there and suddenly he roared, "Silence, there, between decks!"

The doctor turned to him, "Were you addressing me, sir?" he asked, fearlessly. Then he added, "I have only one thing to say to you. If you keep on drinking rum, the world will soon be rid of a very dirty scoundrel!"

The old fellow's fury was awful. He sprang to his feet, surprisingly quickly, and drew and opened a sailor's clasp knife. Before we knew what was happening he had threatened to pin the good doctor to the wall. He remained quite still and there followed a battle of looks between them. The doctor showed no fear and did not so much as blink an eye. Realizing what kind of man he was the Captain soon knuckled under, lowered his weapon, and went back to his seat, grumbling like a beaten dog.

Black Dog appears and disappears

IT WAS NOT very long after this that there occurred the first of the mysterious events that rid us at last of the Captain.

It was one January morning, very early, a pinching, freezing morning, when the cove was gray with hoare-frost. The Captain had risen earlier than usual and set out for the beach, his cutlass swinging under the broad skirts of his tattered old blue coat, his brass telescope under his arm, and his battered hat tilted back on his head.

I was laying the breakfast table for his return when the parlor door opened, and a man stepped in. I had never set eyes on him before. He was a pale, sly-looking creature, with two fingers missing on his left hand. He was not sailorly, and yet he had a smack of the sea about him.

"Come here, sonny," he said suddenly,

and I took a step nearer, rather warily. "Is this here table for my mate Bill?" he continued, with a most unpleasant leer, although I judged he was trying to act in a pleasant fashion.

"If you mean the Captain," I said, "he is out walking. But yes, this table is for him."

"Then you and me'll just get behind the door, and we'll give old Bill a little surprise," he said. Before I could move he took a firm grip of me and pinned me behind him in the corner, so that we were both hidden by the open door.

He took his cutlass from its hilt and loosened the blade in the sheath. All the time we were waiting there, he kept swallowing as if he had a great lump in his throat.

At last the Captain returned from his wanderings and entered the parlor. He slammed the door behind him, as was his wont and he looked neither left nor right.

"Bill," said the stranger, in a voice that I thought he tried to make big and bold.

The Captain spun around on his heel and faced us, all the brown drained out of his face. Then he gasped, "Black Dog!"

"And who else?" returned the stranger, seemingly more at his ease having seen how his presence had affected the Captain. "Black Dog as ever was, come for to see his

old shipmate Billy." This last he said slyly.

"Now look here," said the Captain, recovering himself a little. "So you've run me down. Well, here I am. Speak up, then. What is it? What do you want?"

Black Dog let go of my arm abruptly, ordering me to bring rum, and I obeyed at once. I left them together, but I could hear their voices grow louder and louder. Then all of a sudden came a tremendous explosion of oaths. Chairs and table crashed to the floor! There was a cry of pain, and the next instant, looking out of the window I saw Black Dog in full flight and the Captain hotly pursuing him. Both had drawn cutlasses, but Black Dog had

blood streaming from his left shoulder.

"Jim," said the Captain breathlessly when he returned. "Rum!" As he spoke he swayed a little and leaned against the wall. When I returned with the rum, I saw with great alarm that he had fallen full length on the floor. My mother came running to find out what the trouble was; and it was a happy relief when Dr. Livesey arrived on his regular visit, for we had no idea what to do with the big man stretched out before us.

The doctor helped me to carry him upstairs and we laid him on his bed.

"He'll recover," Dr. Livesey told me. "But he should lie still for a week. Another stroke will finish him."

The black spot

LATER THAT DAY, I went into the Captain's room. He seemed excited though very weak. "Jim," he croaked, "you're the only one I can trust. You'll bring me just one noggin' of rum, matey, won't you?"

I did my best to refuse, but he got more and more excited and at length, so as to keep him quiet, I did as he asked. After he had gulped the rum down, far from quietening down, he began to protest violently that he could not stay where he was.

"They'll have the black spot on me!" he cried, hysterically. "They want to get what is mine. But I'll trick 'em yet. I'm not afraid of 'em. I'll shake 'em off . . ."

He sank back exhausted and lay silent for a while. Then he spoke again. "Jim," he said at last. "You saw that seafaring man today?"

"Black Dog?" I asked.

"Aye," said the Captain, "Black Dog! He's a bad one, but the others are worse. Now, if they do tip me the black spot, remember it's my old sea-chest they're after. You get on a horse then, and ride to that doctor of yours. Tell him to call out the magistrates and the like. Tell him, he'll need 'em if he's going to get the better of old Flint's crew, all of 'em that's left. I was first mate, I was old Flint's first mate, and I'm the only one as knows the place."

I had no idea what he was talking about. Who was Flint? What 'place' did he know and why was it important? Attempting to grasp at least some of the story, I asked, "But what is the black spot, Captain?"

"That's a summons, lad. I'll tell you if I get it. But you just keep your weather-eye open, Jim, and I'll share with you equals!"

Still completely at a loss to understand, I left him then. Maybe I should have marked more carefully what the Captain

had said, but that very evening my father suddenly died. There was much grief in the inn that night with my poor mother in desperate need of comfort, which I tried to give, although I felt in need of some myself. In consequence, I scarcely gave the Captain a thought.

It was a day or so later and a foggy frosty afternoon when we buried my father. I was standing at the door full of sad thoughts and fears for the future when, suddenly, I looked up and saw someone coming down the road. It was obvious that he was blind, for he tapped before him with a stick and wore a great green shade over his eyes and nose. He was all hunched up as if with age, and he had on a huge old tattered sea cloak with a hood, that made him appear deformed. Never in my life had I seen a more dreadful-looking figure.

He stopped in front of me and in an odd sing-song voice, called out, "Will any kind friend inform a poor blind man where, or in what part of this country he may now be?"

"You're at the 'Admiral Benbow,' Black Hill Cove," said I, haltingly.

"I hear a voice," he said, "and 'tis a young voice! Will you give me your hand and lead me in?"

I held out my hand, and the horrible, soft-spoken, eyeless creature gripped it immediately. I noticed at once I was held as if in a vice. I was so startled that I struggled to get free, but the blind man pulled me close.

"Now, boy," he said in a slow, dreadful voice, "take me in to the Captain."

As he spoke he gave my arm such a cruel wrench that I cried out. "The Captain is

The poor Captain's expression when he saw the blind beggar was one of sheer terror. He made to rise, but the blind man said, "Stay where you are, Bill. Now hold out your right hand. Boy, take him by his right hand by the wrist and bring him nearer to my right." And all the time, he never released his grip on my arm.

We both obeyed him to the letter, and I saw him press something from the hollow of the hand that held his stick into the palm of the Captain's.

"Now that's done," said the blind man, and he let me go. Then, with incredible swiftness, he limped out of the parlor into the road and, as I stood motionless, I could hear his stick go tap-tap-tapping into the distance.

At length I dared to look at the Captain. "Ten o'clock!" he cried, staring down at the black spot in the palm of his hand. "Six hours. We'll do 'em yet!" And he sprang to his feet.

Even as he did so, he reeled around, put his hand to his throat and then with a peculiar sound, fell face foremost on the floor.

I ran to him at once, calling to my mother. But haste was all in vain. The Captain was stone dead.

not himself these days since his last stroke. He sits always with a drawn cutlass . . ."

"March!" interrupted the blind man. And I never heard a voice so cruel and cold. "Lead me straight up to him and when I'm in view, cry out, 'Here's a friend for you, Bill.' If you don't . . ." And he gave my arm another twist, "I'll break it."

Utterly terrified, I opened the parlor door, and cried out the words he had ordered, in a trembling voice.

The sea chest

A S SOON AS I had told my mother all that had happened, we lost no time in deciding to go for help. The Captain still owed us much money and she was determined to have it out of the old sea-chest for, as she said, it was rightly hers. Our nearest neighbors were not far away, and the sight of the lighted windows and the sound of human voices acted like a tonic to us both. But our spirits were soon dashed, for no sooner had we told them our troubles and mentioned the name of Flint, than not a man among them made an offer to come back with us to the inn.

"If none of you dare to return with us," cried my mother at last, "then we'll go back alone, Jim and me, for there's money owing to us from the Captain, and I've made up my mind to have it."

As we slipped along the hedges, noiseless and swift, a full moon was beginning to rise. As soon as we were inside the inn I bolted the door fast behind us.

The Captain lay where we had left him. As I knelt down beside him once more, I saw on the floor a little round of paper, blackened on one side. As I examined it, I saw that on the other side were printed the words, "You have till ten tonight."

"That means they won't be back till ten," I told my mother. "It gives us four clear hours." Then I felt in his pockets for the key to his sea-chest; it was not there, but I found it hanging around his neck on a piece of tarry string.

"I'll take nothing but what is due to us," said my mother when, at last, we had unlocked the chest and thrown it open. As we stared down at its contents, however, it seemed there was nothing of great value.

There was a suit of clothes on top. Underneath were sticks of tobacco, a variety of trinkets, some curious West Indian shells and an old Spanish watch, all of which my mother impatiently put on one side. Almost at the bottom, however, she came upon a bundle of what looked like papers, tied up in oilcloth. Next to this was a canvas bag, and as I picked it up there came a sound of gold pieces jingling.

"I'll show these rogues that I'm an honest woman," said my mother firmly, as she began to count over the doubloons and guineas and pieces of eight the bag contained.

"Mother," I urged, "take the whole lot and let's be gone." But my mother, frightened though she was, refused to take more than her due, and we were still arguing when suddenly we both heard a low whistle coming from the hill. That was enough for both of us and as we jumped to our feet, my mother said, "I'll take what I have here and no more."

I picked up the oilskin packet. "Maybe this will help to square the account," I thought, and stuffing it in my pocket, I ran to the door and quickly drew back the great bolts.

We had not got far before we heard clearly the sound of running footsteps, and could see lights from the lanterns the men carried. By the time we got to the little bridge I was certain we would be seen. We had to stay there, however, and I helped my mother down the bank. Then we crouched low beneath the parapet, hardly daring to breathe, but at least we were within earshot of the inn.

As soon as I dared, I left my mother and crept back onto the bank. I crouched down again, but now I could get a clear view of

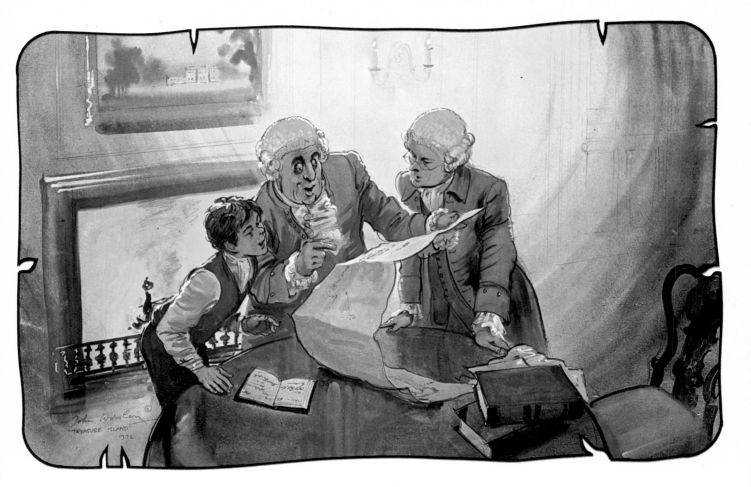

both the 'Admiral Benbow' and the road.

That instant over the brow of the hill they came, seven or eight of them, including the blind beggar, tapping along with the rest. I heard his voice above the others, screaming, "Down with the door!" They rushed the door together and were inside before I had time to draw breath.

The blind beggar had stayed where he was on the road and, presently, one of his mates shouted to him from the doorway. "He's dead, Pew! The Captain's dead and we've found the chest, but they've been here before us . . ."

"Have you got it?" Pew shouted hoarsely. "Have you got Flint's chart?"

After a long pause and a good deal of stamping and cursing, the answer came back. "It's not here. It's not to be found!"

Pew seemed beside himself with rage. "It's that boy!" he screamed. "I should have put out his eyes when I had the chance. Scatter, lads, and find 'em. They can't be far. After them, I say."

Who knows what would have happened to us if the villains had not begun to drink and then quarrel amongst themselves! As it was, they were ill-prepared for the four

or five riders who suddenly came in sight and swept at full gallop towards the inn. Pew turned with a shrill scream and ran, with no one to guide him, straight towards the nearest of the galloping horses. Its rider tried to swerve to avoid him, but in vain. Down he went, and the four hoofs trampled him without mercy. He rolled once onto his side, then collapsed upon his face, and moved no more. Pew was dead, stone dead.

I leapt to my feet and hailed the riders. They were revenue officers, who had been told of our plight by the neighbors and had ridden swiftly to our aid. But by now, the remaining blackguards had all plunged into the surrounding darkness. When we returned to the inn we found it completely wrecked. Standing there with a heavy heart, I thought that we were all but ruined.

"What were they after?" asked the officer-in-charge.

"I think I know, sir," I answered, and I showed him the package of papers. "If you are agreeable, however, I would like to put it in Dr. Livesey's hands."

Dr. Livesey was not at his own house, but on being told he was dining with the

Squire up at the hall, I resolved to go there immediately. Squire Trelawney, with his bluff red face and thick, black eyebrows had always filled me with awe, but standing before him and the good doctor, I forgot my fear of him.

I told the two men my story as clearly as I could and at the end of it Dr. Livesey said, "If Jim agrees, we'll open the packet at once."

The content of the packet was a book and a sealed paper. That was all — but it was more than enough, for the book turned out to be an almost complete record of the infamous Captain Flint's notorious piracy on the high seas. The paper was the map of an island, with latitude and longitude markings, soundings, names of hills, bays and inlets, and every particular that would be needed to bring a ship to a safe anchorage upon its shores. The island was shaped like a sort of fat dragon, and judging from the scale was about nine miles long and five across. It had two fine land-locked harbors, and a hill in the center part called 'The Spy-glass.'

There were several additions that appeared to be of a later date, but above all, three crosses in red ink, two of which were on the north part of the island. But it was the one in the south-west that held our attention most, for against this, in a small neat hand, were the words, 'Bulk of treasure here.'

"Livesey," cried the Squire, after careful study of the map. "You will give up your wretched practice at once. Tomorrow I start for Bristol. In three weeks' time, we'll have the best ship manned by the choicest crew in England. Then we'll sail for Treasure Island. You, Jim Hawkins, shall be the cabin-boy!"

Meeting with Long John Silver

IT WAS NOT until I came to say goodbye to my mother that I realized the full extent of my good fortune. She, for her part, shared something of my joyful and excited mood. The Squire had made good provision for her, and the inn was now all shipshape.

Squire Trelawney had written from Bristol that old Redruth, his faithful gamekeeper, was to accompany me on the journey and was, in fact, to be a member of the ship's crew. My mother was at least thankful that I had a travelling companion.

I am ashamed to say that the events of the past few weeks took their toll and I slept half the journey away despite the fact that I was so looking forward to the adventure.

I awoke with Redruth nudging me. "We've arrived," he said, and almost at once I could smell the tar and salt in the air.

Squire Trelawney was waiting for us in front of a large inn. He was all dressed out like a sea-officer in stout blue cloth, and he greeted us with a smile on his face.

"Here you are!" he cried. "And the Doctor came last night from London. Bravo! The ship's company is complete."

"Oh, sir," I cried, unable to contain my excitement, "when do we sail?"

"Sail?" says he. "We sail tomorrow!"

After we had breakfasted at the inn, the Squire gave me a note addressed to John Silver, or Long John, as he affectionately was called.

"He's lost a leg, Jim," he told me, "but with his help I've got together the toughest old salts imaginable, not pretty to look at maybe, but with grand spirits and considerable experience. And as for the ship herself — you never saw a sweeter schooner, two hundred tons — name *Hispaniola* . . ."

I ran all the way to the inn where apparently Long John Silver was the landlord. It was easy enough to pick him out once I was inside. His left leg was cut

company — for he proposed he showed me the ship — I was his friend for life.

When we reached the *Hispaniola* and stepped aboard, we were saluted by the mate, Mr. Arrow, a brown old sailor, with gold earrings, and a squint. Then I was shown the cabin and presently I was introduced to the ship's Captain. Captain Smollett was a slim, sharp-looking man, who looked me over without saying a word.

The Doctor and the Squire came aboard shortly after, and it was soon plain to me that the captain had a grievance.

"I was engaged," he said, addressing himself to the Squire, "to sail this ship under what we call 'sealed orders.' But now I find that every man before the mast knows more than I do. And further, I learn now that we're going after treasure. I don't like treasure voyages, and I don't like them, above all, when they are supposed to be secret!"

Squire Trelawney's face flushed an angry red at this, and it took all the Doctor's tact to calm matters between them.

However, it was finally agreed that all the arms and powder on board should be kept under lock and key in the stern part of the ship, and closely guarded by men the Squire could personally vouch for.

off, close to the hip, and under the left shoulder was lodged a wooden crutch. But he looked so smiling and moved with such ease among the customers that I didn't even think to pity him for having only one leg.

"Mr. Silver, sir?" I said, going up to him and holding out the note.

"Yes, my lad," said he, "such is my name to be sure. And who may you be?"

Before I had time to answer, he had taken the note and was reading it.

"Ah," he said, "our new cabin-boy!" And he took my hand in his large firm grasp. Just at that very moment one of the customers rose hastily and made for the door. He was outside in a flash, but not before I had recognized him.

"Stop him! Stop him!" I cried. "It's Black Dog!"

"After him, Harry," shouted Long John to one of the men clearing away the glasses. "He hasn't paid his dues . . ."

The man returned before long, but without the rogue. In his absence, Long John, with his hand on his heart, had spent much time swearing he had never seen Black Dog in his life until that very morning. And I — in my innocence — believed him.

After that, we got on famously together and by the time I left the tavern in his

We sail at last

WHEN THE anchor was up and the sails beginning to draw, I knew that the *Hispaniola* had at last begun her voyage to the Island where lay the treasure.

I am not going to relate the voyage in detail, but here I must say something of Long John Silver, who had taken up office as the ship's cook. All the crew respected and even obeyed him, and to me he was

unfailingly kind, always glad to see me in the galley, which he kept as clean as a new pin; the brightly burnished pots and pans hanging up, and his parrot in a cage in one corner.

"Come away, Jim," he would say. "Come and have a yarn with old John. Sit you down and hear the news and a tale or two. Here's Cap'n Flint to tell you we're headin' for a successful voyage."

Captain Flint was the name of his great parrot and the bird, whenever I appeared, would say, "Pieces of eight! — Pieces of eight! — Pieces of eight!" with great rapidity until Long John would throw his handkerchief over the cage and thus silence the bird.

We had some heavy weather on the voyage, which only proved the qualities of the *Hispaniola*. Every man on board

seemed well content and in good spirits, as we sailed steadily along. Our ship rolled evenly, and we were all conscious that we were approaching the last days of our voyage.

Just after sundown one night, when my duties were finished, it occurred to me that I should like an apple. I climbed up on deck, and got bodily into the deep apple barrel, which had been full at the beginning of the voyage, only to find there was scarcely an apple left. But sitting down there in the dark, what with the sound of the waters and the rocking movement of the ship, I had either fallen asleep, or was on the point of doing so, when a heavy man sat down close by.

The barrel shook as he leaned against it, and I was just about to jump up when the man began to speak. It was Silver's voice and, before I had heard a dozen words, I understood that the lives of all the honest men aboard were in danger and now depended on me alone.

"No, no," said Silver, as if in answer to some question I had not heard. "Flint was Cap'n. I was Quartermaster. It was on one of those voyages that I lost my leg, the very

same as old Pew lost his deadlights. Where's all Flint's men now, you ask? Well I'll tell you. Most of 'em are aboard this ship, except old Pew, that is, and he's dead now and under hatches . . ."

There was a pause and then a bright eager voice, I recognized as the voice of the youngest of the crew, began to praise old Silver for his exploits as a pirate.

"Well," returned Long John, "you may be right for I tell you, even Flint was afeared of me. And Flint was the very devil himself."

"Well," said that eager young voice again, "you can count on me, John, and the rest of us for that matter. We're with you — all the way."

"Smart you are," answered Silver, "and a fine gentleman of fortune you'll make when the treasure is ours and you gets your share."

"Here's to old Flint," cried another of the men. "And to the treasure!"

It was clear the villains were well supplied with rum and were beginning to drink freely. But presently, as I crouched inside the barrel, trembling all over with fear, I heard the voice of the Coxswain, Israel Hands say, "I've had almost enough of that Cap'n. Just let me get at him."

"All in good time," answered the Cook. "But meanwhile you'll speak soft and keep sober. And when the time comes you can have the Cap'n, and I will have Trelawney. I'll wring his head off his body with these very hands."

Then they began to toast each other in rum, and Silver broke into a sailor's song, which was only interrupted when the voice of the look-out shouted, "Land-ho!"

I could hear the great rush of feet across the deck and, taking advantage of the general confusion, I slipped out of the barrel and dived behind the fore-sail. From there I made my way, seemingly casually, towards the stern where Dr. Livesey stood. It was impossible to describe what I felt as I saw the villainous Long John Silver draw near to me.

"Ah," he said, in his usual pleasant tone, "this is a sweet spot, this island ahead of us. I knows it well for I've watered there with a trader I was cook in." Then he clapped me upon the shoulder and hobbled away.

"Get the Captain and the Squire down to the cabin," I whispered to the Doctor, "I have some terrible news."

The island of treasure

WHEN, AT LAST, the opportunity came for me to tell the Squire, the Doctor and Captain Smollett all that I had overheard, they received the news comparatively calmly.

The Captain immediately began to weigh up the odds. "We are seven against nineteen," he said, "and we can't turn back. Whatever we do, we must go about our business as if nothing was amiss. The blackguards must not suspect that we know of their dastardly plans."

"Jim here," said the doctor, "can help us more than anyone. The men are not shy with him, and Jim is a noticing lad."

"Hawkins, I put great faith in you," said the Squire, gravely. "Meantime we must prepare to land in the morning."

The next day, Long John stood by the steersman. He knew the passage to the

small natural harbor at the rear of the island like the back of his hand and, under his direction, we sailed close in to shore and dropped anchor.

The heat was sweltering and the men grumbled and cursed as they went about their work — that is, all except Long John, who was as cheerful and obliging as ever. But scarcely for a single moment did he take his eyes off that gray island with its gray-colored woods and tall pine trees that stretched upwards into a gray sky.

It soon became evident that if the men were kept at work much longer, we would all be faced with a mutiny, so at last Captain Smollett went on deck and addressed the crew.

"My lads," he said, "we've had a hot day, and we're all tired. A turn ashore will hurt nobody. So as many as please can go

ashore for the afternoon. I'll fire a gun half-an-hour before sundown as the signal for your return."

I believe the silly fellows thought they would dig up the treasure as soon as they landed on the island, for they immediately stopped cursing and soon Silver had arranged a landing party of thirteen. It was then that I had the idea of going ashore with them and, no sooner did the chance come than I took advantage of it. I slipped over the side and curled up in the fore-sheets of the nearest boat.

No one took the slightest notice of me, though for a moment I thought Silver had seen me from his boat. He did, I think, see me when our boat landed, but I swung myself ashore by means of an overhanging branch, and ran through the thick foliage

as fast as I could until I was out of shouting range. Pleased that I had given them all the slip, I began to enjoy myself. I crossed a marshy swamp full of willows and bulrushes and, in more open land, I came upon all kinds of flowering plants. Here and there a lazy snake hissed at me with a kind of spinning-top noise.

How long I wandered over the island, I have no idea. But, all at once, a wild duck flew up with a loud quack, and I halted as the whole fen came alive with a great cloud of birds, screaming and circling in the sky.

It was then I heard human voices, still very faint, but coming steadily louder and nearer. Trembling from head to toe and not daring to make a sound, I crawled under cover of the nearest thick bush and waited. From my concealed vantage point I soon saw that the voices belonged to Long John Silver and Tom, one of the younger members of the crew, whom I had always rather liked.

Suddenly I heard Tom cry out, "As for you, John Silver, you've been a mate of mine in the past, but you're a mate no more. If I'm to die like a dog, I'll die in my

duty. Kill me, if you can, but I defy you and your wicked doings."

He turned to walk away, but before he could take a dozen steps, I saw Silver seize the branch of a tree to support himself. Then whipping the crutch from under his arm, he sent it hurtling through the air. It struck poor Tom with stunning force, and he gave a sort of gasp as he dropped to the ground.

Silver had hopped to him in a flash and, before I could even draw breath, he had buried his knife in poor Tom's defenseless body.

I do not know what it rightly is to faint, but I do know that for the next little while the whole world swam away from me in a whirling mist. When I came to myself again, the monster had his crutch under his arm and his hat upon his head. He brought out a whistle from his pocket and blew upon it. When I heard it, I knew that more men would be coming and I might be discovered.

With this in mind and trembling with fright, I crawled away farther into the woods. And, as soon as I was clear of the thicket, I ran as I had never run before, without taking any notice of where I was going.

Old man of the island

IN MY TERROR I had covered a great deal of ground, when suddenly something brought me to a dead halt. There was a creature just ahead of me. I changed my direction, twisting and turning in and out of the tall pine trees, but it had turned too and was following me. And when at last I could run no more, it advanced towards me.

It was then that I saw it was a man, but quite the strangest I had ever set eyes upon. His skin was burnt black by the sun, even to his lips, and his blue eyes made such a startling contrast in that black face that they will surely haunt me for the rest of my days. He was dressed in rags roughly made from an old ship's canvas, fastened together by a variety of brass buttons, bits of stick and loops of dried goatskin. All this was held in place by an old and very broad brass-buckled leather belt.

"Who are you?" I asked, trying to hide my trembling.

"Benn Gunn," he answered, and his voice sounded hoarse and awkward, like a rusty lock which hasn't been used for many a year.

"I'm poor Ben Gunn, I am, and I haven't spoken with a Christian these three years."

"Three years!" I cried. "Were you shipwrecked then?"

"No, lad," said he, "marooned — marooned I was, three years ago and since then I've lived on goats and berries and oysters. You don't happen to have a piece of cheese about you, do you? No? Pity it is, many's the long night I've dreamed of cheese, toasted, mostly."

"If ever I can get on board again," I said, "you shall have as much cheese as you can eat."

When I saw that the poor man was

harmless, I set about telling him who I was, and about the *Hispaniola*.

Ben cowered away from me when I told him Silver was one of Flint's men.

"A man with a wooden leg?" he gasped, a look of fear crossing his blackened face.

"The very same," I told him. "And with the others he's after the treasure that Captain Flint must have buried on this island."

At this the fear left Ben Gunn's face and something like a smile took its place.

"Put your trust in old Ben Gunn," he said. "I'm rich, rich, rich!" He looked at me as if he had a dark secret to share but could not bring himself to tell me. "I'll tell you what," he went on, after a pause, "I were in Flint's ship when he buried the treasure. He and six strong seamen went ashore. But when he comes back to the ship, he was all alone. How he had done it, not a man aboard could make out."

"Why did you stay here, Ben?" I asked.

"'Twas three years ago," said Ben, sidling up to me and pinching my arm. 'Twas on another ship, see, and I tells them about the treasure. Twelve days they look for it and not finding it, out of spite they left me here with a spade and pickaxe."

As he finished speaking, the thunder of a cannon shook the whole island.

"They've begun to fight!" I shouted. "Follow me!" And I began to run towards the anchorage, my fears all forgotten.

Suddenly, and not more than a quarter of a mile in front of us, I saw the Union Jack fluttering above a thicket of trees.

Inside the stockade

IT WAS ONLY afterwards that I learned from the Doctor all that had happened after I had slipped away from the *Hispaniola*. It seemed that when my absence was discovered, the Doctor with Hunter, a man he could trust, had made up his mind to go ashore and search for me.

They had made for the stockade, a stout log-house, around which stood a fence six feet high. Although it was marked most accurately on Flint's old map they had come upon it, "almost unexpectedly," the Doctor said, close to the shore.

The Doctor had realized in an instant what an advantage his small party would have if they could take immediate possession of the house. And, with this in mind, they returned to the ship.

By now, the mutineers still on board were three parts drunk and fully occupied in waiting for the return of their leader, Long John Silver. This made the task of getting away from the ship unnoticed a good deal easier.

In all, my friends managed to make five trips, loading the small boats with provisions, gear and ammunition. On the last trip of all, some of the mutineers came to their senses and began firing. Captain Smollett, however, kept his head, although their boat was upturned, and they all managed to reach the stockade without loss of life or sustaining injury.

You can imagine with what interest I heard their story and how eagerly they listened to mine. I told them about old Ben Gunn and how, when I saw the Union Jack flying above the stockade, I had succeeded, with his help, in making an entrance under cover of darkness.

Even as I spoke, shots rang out and the Squire informed me, with a cheerfulness I'm sure he didn't feel, that we were

surrounded on all fronts by the mutineers.

"But time and rum are on our side," he added, still putting on a great show of spirit.

If we had been allowed to sit idle, we should all have had too much time to think and would soon have become despondent, but Captain Smollett divided us into watches. Every time we had an opportunity for a crack at the enemy we were to take it. But it should be undertaken with extreme care, as at all costs we must save our own lives.

According to the Captain, we had all the advantages, having most of the stores and a good number of the muskets.

After my watch I was dead tired, and when I got to sleep at last, I slept like a log of wood. I was awakened suddenly by a hustle and bustle and the sound of voices.

"Flag of truce!" I heard someone say, and then immediately after, with a cry of surprise, "Silver himself!"

At that, up I jumped and, rubbing my eyes, ran to a small knot hole in the wall.

Sure enough, there were two men just

outside the stockade, one of them waving a
white cloth. The other, no less a person
than Silver himself, was standing quietly
beside him.

"Keep indoors, men," warned Captain
Smollett. "Ten to one this is a trick."

Then he hailed the buccaneer.

"Who goes there? Stand, or we fire," he
called.

"Flag of truce!" cried Silver.

"And what do you want with your flag of
truce?" returned the Captain.

This time it was the other man who
replied.

"Cap'n Silver, sir, to come aboard and
make terms," he shouted.

"Cap'n Silver! Don't know the man.
Who is he?" the Captain shouted back.

"Me, sir," cried Long John, in a smooth

voice. "We're willing to submit, if we can come to terms."

"If you want to parley," cried the Captain, "you'll have to come closer."

Silver had terrible hard work getting across the soft sand, but he stuck to it like a man of guts, and at last arrived before the captain. He saluted handsomely. He was decked out in his best; an immense blue coat, thick with brass buttons, hanging as low as his knees, and a fine laced hat, set on the back of his head.

"You come no further," ordered Captain Smollett. "And if you have anything to say, you had best say it and be done with it."

"Right you are, Cap'n Smollett," replied Silver, sitting down on the sand. "We want the treasure and we'll have it. You would just as soon save your lives, I reckon, and we'll grant them to you. You have the chart. We need it to find the treasure. So you give us the chart, and we'll give you the chance of coming aboard along of us, with safe passage."

Captain Smollett looked at him calmly and began to fill a pipe. "Is that all?" he asked.

"Every last word, by thunder," answered Silver. "Refuse, and you've seen the last of me; from now on, it'll be musket-balls."

"Very good," said the Captain. "Now, you listen to me. The wisest choice you can make, for you can't sail the ship, is to come to me unarmed when I'll clap you all in irons and take you home to a fair trial in England."

With a dreadful oath, and a threat that made my blood run cold, Silver struggled to his feet and plunged forward over the sand, disappearing among the trees.

Not a bough waved, not the gleam of a musket-barrel betrayed the presence of our foes, yet we knew they were all there, surrounding us in the trees.

The attack

THERE WAS not much time left to us to arrange our defenses, although we all rallied around as quickly as we could. Suddenly, with a loud huzza, a band of the pirates leapt from the woods on the north side, and ran straight on the stockade. At that moment, the fire was once more opened from another part of the woods, to distract our attention. A rifle-ball sang through the doorway, and blew the Doctor's musket to pieces.

The pirates swarmed over the fence like monkeys. The Squire and one of his men, Gray, fired again and again. Three of the buccaneers fell, but four others were upon us, and it was only the smoke-filled log-house that saved us from complete slaughter.

"Out lads! Quick!" cried the Captain. "Hands on your cutlasses!"

I snatched a cutlass and dashed for the door. Somebody aimed a blow at me and I leaped to one side, missing my footing in the soft sand and rolling headlong down the slope. When I returned to the log-house, it was to find we had beaten them off.

Disquieting words from the Squire greeted me. "The Captain's wounded," he said, "an' we're like to lose two men, so badly wounded are they." Then he made an effort to sound more hopeful. "But we've won the first round."

After dinner that night, I saw the Doctor consult long and earnestly with Squire Trelawney. Then he took his hat and pistols, strapped on a cutlass, put the

chart in his pocket, and slipped out of the enclosure on the north side.

"It's all right," the Squire reassured us. "He's off to try and meet with Ben Gunn."

I watched him go with envy in my heart and, presently, when the others were

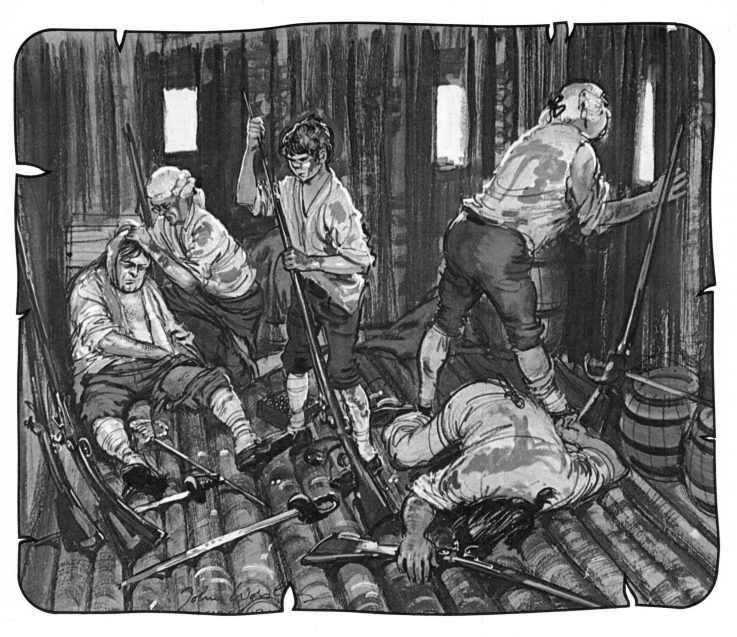

engaged with their weapons, I took hold of a brace of pistols, and made a bolt for it over the stockade. In seconds I was making my way stealthily through the thick trees. My plan was simple; I had in mind to find Ben Gunn's boat, for in the course of conversation, he had told me where it lay. Then, under cover of darkness, I would make for the *Hispaniola* and cut her adrift.

It was a night out of ten thousand to defy my purpose, for a dense fog had settled on Treasure Island and there was absolute blackness all around. Yet, by great good fortune and surprisingly swiftly, I came upon Ben's boat. It was more like a coracle, the kind made by the ancient Britons, than a proper boat, and it was not without difficulty that I got it launched into the water with myself inside.

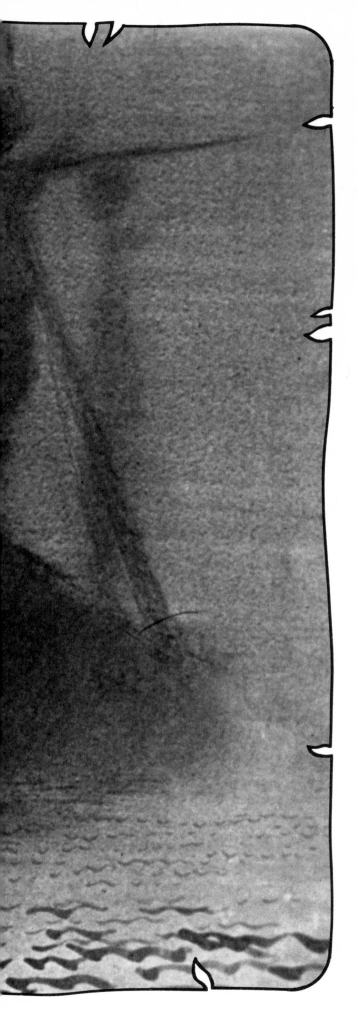

My sea adventure

GOOD FORTUNE stayed with me. The tide carried me strongly, straight towards the *Hispaniola,* and as the clouds parted, allowing the moon to shine through and pick out her shimmering silhouette, my heart pounded. As my bobbing boat came alongside of her a puff of wind suddenly forced the ship into the right position for me to lean out and cut two or three strands of the thick rope that held her at anchor.

As I rested for a moment, I heard voices from the deck. Israel Hands, one of the treacherous rogues, and another of the crew were arguing violently. But then, the breeze stiffened once more and I was able to cut through the last of the fibers. At the same moment, the schooner began spinning slowly across the current.

For the first time, I saw my fool-hardiness, for now I was in danger of being smashed to pieces should she catch my boat with her sturdy bow. My only chance was to grasp the light cord that railed over-

board and pull myself upwards. With infinite caution I did just that, until I had a fair view of the deck and a portion of the cabin's interior.

By now, the schooner had righted herself and was gliding pretty swiftly through the water. As the wind changed again, I tumbled head first on the deck. I saw the only two watchmen who had been left on board. One lay as stiff as a handspike and the other, Israel Hands himself, his face as white as candle wax, was propped against the bulwarks. I thought he was dead too, until he shifted his position with a low moan.

"I've come aboard, Mr. Hands," I said, "to take possession of this ship."

He looked at me sourly but said nothing. So I left him there and, dodging the boom, ran to the color lines. With a triumphant feeling I hauled down the black flag of the buccaneers, and threw it overboard.

"God save the King!" I shouted, waving my cap. "And there's an end to the Jolly Roger."

Then I went back to Israel Hands, who had regained a bit of color and seemed altogether much stronger.

"Now look here, Cap'n Hawkins," he began, leering at me in a false attempt at being friendly, "you give me food and drink and an old scarf to tie up my wounds, and I'll show you how to sail the ship."

"I'll tell you one thing," I said. "I mean to get her into the North Inlet and beach her there."

"So you shall," said Hands in a comradely way. "An' I'll be the one to help you."

So the bargain with Hands was struck and when he asked me to fetch him some wine, I left him untied, for he was groaning at intervals most convincingly all the time we spoke.

After he had drunk the wine, he told me to put the helm hard up. This I did and the *Hispaniola* swung round rapidly heading

straight for the low wooded shore. The excitement of having brought the good ship soundly into port, as it were, threw me off my guard. When next I looked

eyes, then his right hand went back over his shoulder. The same second something sang through the air. I felt a blow and then a sharp pain through my shoulder. I was pinned to the mast by the long knife Hands had thrown. My hands jerked without my knowing it, causing my pistols to go off with an ear-shattering report. The pain was acute as I wrenched myself free, in time to see Hands, with a horrible cry, plunge head first into the sea. Wearily I climbed down, but now, my only thought was to get back to the Squire and tell him that the schooner was safe, and ready for all of us to sail her home.

round, there was Hands, already halfway towards me, with a knife in his right hand. I left hold of the tiller with a cry of sheer terror and this, I imagine, saved my life, for the tiller struck Hands across the chest and halted him in his stride.

Yet he recovered quickly enough, and as he chased after me, I felt the ship stagger as she struck ground. Then she canted over to portside. We were both thrown to the deck, but I was first up, and I sprang into the mizzen shrouds. I did not draw breath till I was seated on the cross-trees.

Hands glared up at me with blazing

Pieces of eight

WHEN I REACHED the shore, I set off for the stockade in high spirits. The moon's silver beam had once more disappeared behind dark clouds and so I had to grope my way into the log-house. I was anxious not to rouse my sleeping friends, at least until I had taken up my position.

Then, all at once, a shrill voice came at me out of the darkness, "Pieces of eight! Pieces of eight!"

I would have recognized that voice anywhere. It came from Silver's green parrot! I jumped up, but there was no time to escape. In a matter of seconds I was held fast. One of the buccaneers brought a lighted brand and, in the red glare of the torch, I saw I was held by Long John himself, still in his blue suit although it was now stained with blood. We were both surrounded by six of the buccaneers.

"I always liked you, Jim," he said, holding me fast. "Sold you down the river they 'ave, those fancy friends of yours. Think you're a traitor, the way you nipped off and left 'em."

"They do not!" I cried defiantly, wondering at the same time where the Doctor and the Squire could be.

I was soon to find out, for Long John told me that he had bargained most cunningly with them for possession of the log house and all its stores, in return for their free access to the shore.

"Kill me if you please!" I began again, after a long pause. "But I've brought the schooner to a place you'll never find!"

One of the buccaneers sprang towards me with a terrible oath and would have knifed me on the spot if Silver hadn't cried, "Stop there!" His eyes ablaze he glared around at his men, who were muttering rebelliously among themselves. "You won't touch the lad as long as I'm here," he said, keeping me close and looking slowly around him. Then he continued,

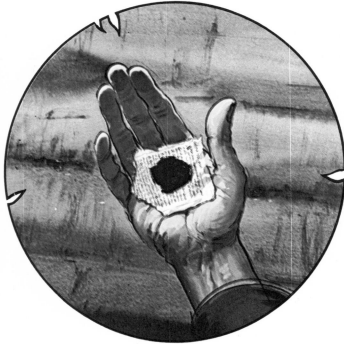

"Do any of you gentlemen want to have it out with me now? Well, come on then, I'm ready!"

Not a man moved towards him and then one by one, they turned away and stumbled towards the door. It was then I noticed that some of them were wounded.

"They're thinking to throw me over, Jim," said Silver, when the last of them had disappeared. "But there's never a hope for 'em."

"You mean you've given up?" I asked.

"I do," said John Silver, deliberately. "When I saw that the schooner was gone, I gave up. Now, if you stand by me, you can save old John from swinging. I'm on your side now."

When the men returned, they huddled together just inside the door as if they were afraid. Then one of their number came forward and pressed something into Silver's hand.

"So it's the black spot for me is it?" said he quietly, looking down at the circle of paper in his palm.

"You're finished, Silver," growled one of the pirates. "We've had enough of you. You're deposed."

But Long John had yet another trick up his sleeve. "Finished, am I?" he said slyly. And he cast down to the floor a piece of paper that I recognized instantly. It was the map with the three red crosses, the very same that I had found in the oilcloth and given to the Doctor so long ago.

Silver pulled himself upright, watching the men closely. "So you lost the ship, an' I found the treasure," he said at last. "Who's the better man, I ask ye all?"

"Long John Silver!" they shouted, staring down at the piece of paper on the floor. "Silver forever!"

The rest of the night passed quietly enough and, in the morning, to my astonishment Dr. Livesey himself appeared at the log-house, armed with medicines and bandages. Apart from a start of recognition, he paid me no attention, but began at once to tend some of the wounded pirates.

"We're most humbly grateful to you, Doctor," said Long John at last. "An' providing young Hawkins here will give me his solemn word not to slip the cable, then I'm agreeable for you and he to parley."

I gave my promise at once and Silver then requested the Doctor to step outside and wait for us beyond the stockade.

"You tell him, boy, tell him as how I saved your life," Silver whispered, as he led me out. And I nodded. Then he settled himself down on a stump of a tree, well out of earshot but not taking his eyes off me for a moment as I walked towards the Doctor.

"So, Jim," said the Doctor, as I went up to him, "here you are. Heaven knows I can't find it in my heart to blame you, but it was downright cowardly to run away . . ."

At these cruel words, I own that I could not hold back my tears. "Doctor," I whispered finally, "my life is forfeit anyway, but not for the reason you might think. Part by luck and part by risk, I got to the ship, and now she lies beached in North Inlet . . ."

"The ship!" exclaimed the Doctor, his whole face lighting up. "Jim, Jim, every step you took was but to save our lives. And we have misjudged you sorely! Jump the fence, lad, quickly and away with me."

"I gave my word," I said, "I must go back."

"Go then," said the doctor, "but don't lose heart." He dressed the wound in my shoulder and then raising his voice he shouted, "Silver, if you keep the boy close behind you and look after him, then upon my soul, I'll do my best to keep you from the gallows."

The treasure hunt

WE MUST have been a curious sight, if anyone had been there to see us, as later that morning we set out on the quest for that treasure — the treasure that had been the cause of all the events of the last weeks.

Silver had two guns slung about him, and a pistol in each pocket of his long blue coat. To complete his strange appearance, Captain Flint sat perched upon his shoulder and gabbled odds and ends of sea talk. I had a line about my waist and was forced to follow obediently after the Cook, who held the loose end of rope between his powerful teeth. For all the world I was led like a dancing bear.

The other men were burdened with picks and shovels, and some with pork, bread and brandy for their midday meal.

Guided by Silver, who stopped now and then to study the map, we came at last within sight of the hill called the Spyglass. The party spread out then, in a fan shape, shouting and striding to and fro. A good

way behind the rest, Silver and I followed, I still tethered by my rope, he hopping forward among the sliding gravel, his breath coming in hoarse pants at the effort.

Suddenly, the man to the left of us began to cry aloud, as if in terror. Shout after shout came from him, and the others began to run in his direction.

"He can't have found the treasure," Silver muttered and indeed, when we reached the spot where the man stood, trembling, we saw that it was not treasure he had come upon, but a human skeleton. The way the skeleton lay, perfectly straight — the feet pointing one direction, the hands, raised above the head, and pointing directly in the opposite — made Silver thoughtful.

"I've a notion," said he, at last, "that this is one of Flint's jokes. He killed 'em all, every man, and this one he must have hauled here and laid down by compass, shiver my timbers! Just take a bearing, will you, along the line of them bones."

This was done and Silver cried, "I thought so! The skeleton is pointing in the direction of the treasure."

The men were quieter and subdued now as we began to climb upwards through the woods until, all at once, out of a thicket of trees before us, came a thin, high, trembling voice.

"Fifteen men on the dead man's chest — Yo-ho-ho, and a bottle of rum!"

I saw the color drain from the men's faces as if by magic. "It's Flint himself!"

cried one of them, in sheer terror.

Then the voice wailed, "Darby M'Graw, fetch aft the rum."

"That's it!" another one gasped. "Old Flint's very last words." I felt sure they would flee that place at once had they not been rooted to the spot in sheer terror.

Still Silver was unconquered. I could hear his teeth rattle in his head, but he had not yet surrendered.

"Come to think on it," he said slowly, "it was like Flint's voice, I grant you. But I think it was like somebody else's voice again. By the powers — Ben Gunn!" he suddenly roared.

Some of the color returned to the men's cheeks at Silver's words, and quick to take advantage of this, he urged them forward. I said nothing, but stumbled on behind, as Silver pulled roughly on the rope.

The men moved on faster now, and Silver doubled his pace to catch up with them. When he reached them, he almost fell back on top of me, so shocked and disappointed was he.

Before us was a huge hole in the ground with the sides fallen in and the grass sprouting on the bottom. In this was the shaft of a spade and the boards of several packing cases. And on one, I saw the name *WALRUS*, the name of Flint's ship. The treasure had been found, but not a gold piece or doubloon was to be seen. The treasure had gone!

The end of the adventure

WITH DESPERATE cries the pirates jumped into the hole and scrabbled about, forlornly but fruitlessly, cursing and swearing to themselves all the while. One by one they climbed out again and bunched together on the opposite side from Silver and myself. Their disappointment and anger was clearly being turned on us and I knew that they meant to put an end to us.

Just then, crack! crack! — crack! Three musket shots flashed out of the thicket, and two of the men spun around and fell into the hole. Long John finished off the third. The remaining buccaneers took to their heels at the moment when the Doctor, Gray — one of the loyal seamen — and Ben joined us, their muskets smoking.

Long John wiped his brow on his dirty sleeve, before turning to the doctor.

"Thank you, kindly," he said, and then to Ben Gunn, "So it's you, Ben Gunn! Well, you're a fine friend to be sure!"

Ben wriggled like an eel at seeing his old shipmate again, but he managed to bring out, "How do, Mr. Silver, pretty well meself, thank you."

As for me, with the Doctor's arm around my shoulder, I felt at peace with myself and the world. We walked together down the hill and he told me how Ben Gunn had discovered Flint's treasure long ago and removed it to a cave in the northeast of the island; and how, as I had guessed, too, the ghost voices had belonged to Ben!

I understood on the instant why the Doctor had delivered up the map to Silver. Because of it and all unwittingly, he had led the men into a well planned ambush.

The next morning we fell early to work, transporting the great mass of gold from Ben's hideout to the beach and from there to the *Hispaniola*. This work went on throughout the following day until a fortune in English, French, Spanish and Portuguese doubloons had been stored away on board.

Silver, I should say, was allowed his liberty, though only poor Ben Gunn treated him with any kind of respect. Of the other pirates, we saw never a sign. But when we sailed away at last, we left a good stock of powder and shot, medicines, food and other necessities on the beach for them to pick up after we had gone.

We were so short of men that everyone on board had to bear a hand, except for the Captain, who was still weak from his wounds. We set a course for the nearest port in Spanish America, for we could not risk the voyage home without fresh hands and more supplies.

It was just at sundown when we cast anchor in a most beautiful land-locked gulf, and we were soon surrounded by shore boats full of friendly Negroes and Mexican Indians.

Leaving Ben Gunn in charge of the ship, with instructions to keep close watch on Silver, we went ashore and had such an agreeable time that day was breaking when we once again came alongside the *Hispaniola*. No sooner had we set foot on deck than Ben Gunn confessed that Silver was gone and had taken part of our treasure with him. Apparently he had cut through a bulkhead unobserved and had removed one of the sacks of coin worth perhaps three or four hundred guineas. No doubt it was meant to help him on his further wanderings. Yet I think we were all pleased to be rid of him so cheaply!

Well, to make a long story short, we got a few hands on board. Then we set sail for home, and after an uneventful journey we reached England's shores once again. All of us had an ample share of the treasure, Ben Gunn getting a thousand pounds which he spent or lost in just three weeks!

As for me, I returned to the 'Admiral Benbow' and my mother. Oxen and wain-ropes would not bring me back to that accursed island; and the worst dreams that ever I have are when I hear the surf booming about its coasts, or start upright in bed, with the sharp voice of Captain Flint still ringing in my ears: "Pieces of eight! Pieces of eight!"